INTERVIEWS

FROM THE

LAST DAYS

Natasha —
See you on
the colony!
Christina
Soave

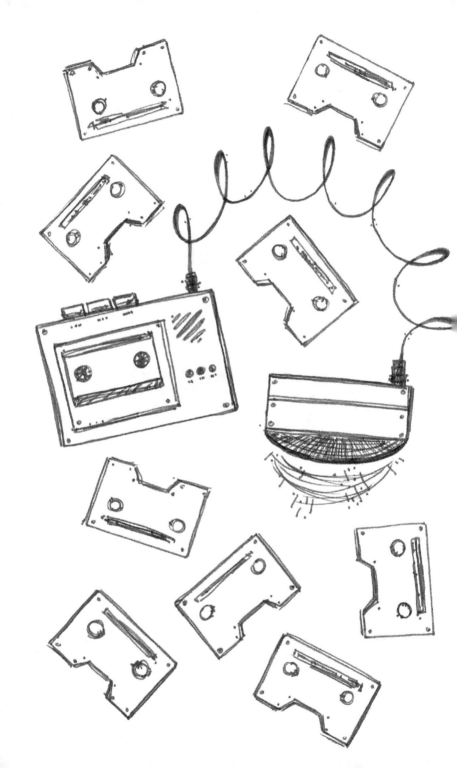

CHRISTINA LORAINE'S

INTERVIEWS

FROM THE

LAST DAYS

atmosphere press

For Holden

That artistic heart and mathematical mind will take
you anywhere. You'll be just fine.

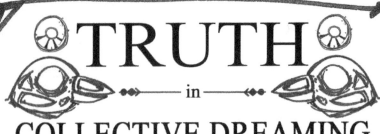

TRUTH
— in —
COLLECTIVE DREAMING
Issue 5 -18 ———————————————— DV 32 -10

Re-assigned soldier
recalls planet full of flora,
claiming military mandated
lobotomy was botched

... argo,"
... n tried it
... eeded salt.
... ation grows
... f sunlight
... colony.

Sun two is almost

Experience reoccurring
dreams of an apocalypse?

TABLE OF CONTENTS

PRELUDE

[The Journalist]

Arriving home
I relinquish reality
for temporal comforts,
double check the deadbolt
drop the faux smile
resume the frown
empty my bag
toss some things on the ground —
stored speculations
laborious lamentations
endless reflections
uncensored pontifications,
off the record run ins
dialogues with denizens,
clandestine conversations
captured on tape —
available to regurgitate
even if it's late.
Rewind
replay
reabsorb —
there's been plenty to record.

I talk to people
record what they say —
journalism

the standard way.
Sure
that's what I do
paid by the line
feeding the teleprompter
writing the words
that'll be read later, live
at five
channel nine.
I'm just a credit
a by-line
no production privileges
no producer pull,
any content
is certainly censorable —
editors endlessly editing,
I'd risk my recycling
discredentialing
reassigning,
jeopardizing a seat
on a flight-ship
off of this desert
out of these ant hills —

What can I possibly do?

It's far too late
for exiting en masse —
the probable outcome
of releasing my tongue

sharing these tapes,
an immediate backlash
direct whiplash
hysteria
panic
congestion in the tunnels,
distress
angst —
no way
to spend your last moments,
but don't think I failed to consider it —
wrestle it through my nightmares
drag it out of bed
schlep it around with me,
hundred pound monstrosity

Yet, others try —
try to warn them
awaken the masses
hoping heaven's
giving out free passes.
They landed on my radar
right around the time
of that major
archeological find,
unsanctioned gatherings
assembly by choice
attempting to warn citizens
of the very things
captured here, on tape.

They've reverted to engraving
carving convincing publications
handing them out
no longer hiding
no longer undercover —
they're shouting this stuff out.

Mostly, no one listens
no one hears
turn a blind ear
there's no protest
no upheavals,
look around you —
rebels
are few
and far between,
planet Vest's majority
clearly enjoys conformity.
Desert Vest
will forever be the land
of government command.

Documentation
preservation
have become my focus —
talking to people
as many as possible
before this whole place
presumably blows
stringing stories together

finding connections,
these aren't just tapes
of people's professions
they're recorded confessions
on the record mentions
singular perspectives
collected
by subversively sidestepping security
sparing
the propaganda-spiked prose
of my daily grind,
I wander everywhere
anyplace
corridors to the spaces
behind the space —
asking people
for a brief moment
just a quick minute
of their time

What job were you assigned?

Professions,
questions centered on careers
job details —
easy ice breakers
on a planet that's never seen ice,
before long
they're shedding clues like burnt skin,
a snapshot of society

gleaned from within

I've been peeling through them
hundreds of encounters
hours of audio
rewind
replay
splicing specifics
gathering, compiling
saving, filing. . .

Planet DV,
home to you and me,
is approaching apocalypse —
let's just be frank about this.

These interviews
may be all that remain
snippets of words: the aftermath of souls,
pieces of the whole —
DIY collection of truth

I'll take these records with me
they'll survive,
granted I make it there on time —
interviews from the last days on Desert Vest
if I've lived for anything,
let it be this.

THE TREE BUILDER

[The Artist]

Weaving crimson
with iron oxide,
I work above our
scorched land
with your throwaways —
your scrap.
Some of us
simply toil in the heat
the unrelenting rays,
while the strongest find ways
of discovering beauty —
visual sonnets.

Welders snatch
any alloy
as long as
it's light enough,
easy to carry to his perch —
his workstation,
any scrap will do because
he's got a job to do.
Day Laborer
in a land that suffers
from two
suns
and too

many workers
surrounded by light,
but unable to see
that our jobs are
really Art —
public installations,
elegance commissioned
under the guise of Progress.

I'm a tree builder, yes
but unlike the others
I choose my metals
for their aesthetic appeal,
for their graceful form —
or their existential grit.
Purposefully selected
with a discerning eye
and piggy-backed up,
to my branch
up high.
I fuse it to the last,
this metallic canopy
growing against the sun,
To spite it, you said —
To take it for all it's worth,
Revenge of the scorched earth.
All of the metal
you stole from the ground
rises up
toward the sky —

growing as we build
piece
after piece,
the twisted forms of trees —
things you said
you read about once.
Parodies of trees
Biological Antichrists —
I weave their branches
and solder their leaves,
One less bit off the ground —
Out of the way, you say.
You've found a method
to generate power
from relentless heat,
the land's
eternal suns
have more to give, you say —
and so
we build upward,
we build out,
levels and layers
branches and leaves —
Trees of Babel.

Have you looked up
to see my work? —
My smooth color
transitions the darkest umber
slowly to

the chromiest of chromes.
Curating your trash
into similar
toned groups,
I'm blind to everything
outside of
Color and Line
as fine-fingered engineers
climb
not far below me —
installing your technology
wiring the trees,
passing among my branches,
the ones I created.
I ask them
if they prefer
Monet over Basquiat —
but they never reply
No one reads science fiction anymore,
except you.

You've been scribbling
blueprints of forests
mapping out electrical grids
and mine shafts,
plotting and planning —
No time to stop
once the ground
has been emptied
and the suns

are finally
fully obstructed —
converted
to electricity,
all according to your plan,
Maybe then
you'll have time
to stop,
pause for a moment
look up
crane your neck
take it all in,
I made it for you —
the reason to see
your forest
for my single tree.

NUMBER FIVE-FIVE

[The Quality Inspector]

Roll'em on down the line —
I'll ensure they fit the specs
Nothing mis-shapen
Nothing mis-formed —
They're just a number, really
fire-forged replicas
the Product
the Sale
Me, I scan them
spot deficiencies
pull the duds
takes a good eye
puts the food on the table
keeps the suns off head,
better than any outside job —
under those dominating rays
The Twin Generals,
their heat campaign
forever assaulting
this bleached planet —

Yes! Anything is better
than working outdoors —
most of the veterans I know
ended up
in surface-level security,

but my retest score
was much higher
enough to keep me underground
and happy to still be around —

I savor my melting years
they roll off me
like machine gun barrels
down my conveyor line,
Redundant Redundancy
clocking in
clocking out
it pays the bills
it covers the rent —
someday I may be promoted,
moved on down the line
End Product Inspector —
Inspected by:
Number Five-Five,
I could afford
to move deeper underground —
a respectable borough
one of those bunker-condos
on the negative-fifty-fifth floor
full amenities
no need to go out,
climate-controlled
Blindly Benign.
Just a few more million barrels
left to inspect

eyes to the front
never look left
thumb just so
fingers bent.
Cylinders of gunmetal,
tens
hundreds
thousands by midday —
Clink-Clink-Clink!
that metallic hollow sound
Identical Complacency
making their way
across my vision —
over in front of me
Consistent Consistency
easy work,
good pay

In this job
I live
get by
see plenty of days,
more than enough time
to try and send my memory
on down the line —
Despite their best tries
at broadband laser lobotomy,
the moment my platoon
returned to DV
is still very fresh to me:

single file
flashing lights —
then those in my rank
couldn't speak quite right
acted like they didn't remember
what we'd done
what we'd seen —
How could anyone forget?
Unless it was the light trick —
the lieutenant neglected to note
that my eyes were closed
saving my memory, but
killing my bond with the military.
Now I'm content to strive for security
mediocrity is fine by me
boring is a superlative for me —
here is where I'm supposed to be
far from the places
these barrels could soon be —

You see,
war is where I learned to cry
when all I ever wanted to be
was a regular guy.

WHITECOATS, MICROSCOPES

[The Food Scientist]

Hi, can I help you
What do you need?
I'm not one for interviews
or needless reprieves
my work is urgent
vital to life
formulating formulas
extrapolating enzymes
I calculate
concise caloric counts —
Whitecoats, Microscopes
compacting your meals
without any "feels."

My technicians calibrate
precise processors
optimal efficiency
efficient optimization —
our reputation
rests
on generations eating
swallowing
consuming
bottle after bottle
tried and true
It worked for them

It'll work for you too.

What?
Surely you joke
please,
save your quotes —
I saw that science-
fiction movie too —
Who came up
with that junk?
It was a complete flunk,
Consumables
grown outdoors
in the air —
alien soft
colors magically bright —
How strange it sounds
out in the light —
no processing
no packaging
they forgot the middleman —
who will compile
the *nutritional file?*
Whitecoats, Microscopes
without us
it's back to the Stone Age for you
chewing on rocks
breaking a tooth

Who has time

for those crazy stories —
B ' movies? *Ha!*
I'd grade far worse,
Why here, we're
Pragmatic Pragmatists —
feet on the ground
Whitecoats, Microscopes
reading scientific periodicals —
Monthly Minerals,
The Quarterly
Rock Quarry
nightly dreams
laced with
Periodic Tables
set for a king
Magnesium Sulfate
Copper Cocktails
premium blend —
crunchy vitamins
starchy rocks
protein pellets —
only the best
directly from
DV sector ten
we ship them in
grind them out —
seal in gell caps
bottle'um out
stamp with a label
a moniker

a name
formed right here,
in house
locally made —
we put all your meals
into mid-sized pills
Natural Food —
the rocks of the land!

Banish childish
agricultural fantasies —
they're poisoning logic
gumming-up your head
negating neuropahways
making it hard for you
to get ahead —
there's no
future in fairytales,
you're old enough to know —
shade your eyes from the suns
stick with the script
take your pills on time,
we develop everything here
and it's always been
just fine.

THE GRIND

[The Machinist]

I operate on vague generalities
wordless soliloquies
emotional liabilities —
What do you want to say to me?
Can you read a face?
Catch a glance?
Sense a vibe?
Get out of this place!

I'm a machinist
fabricating filaments for flight-ships
stuck on the night shift.
Math, engineering — same as everyone
"How enduring!"

Now, let me be.

My shift is done
and I don't want to speak to anyone.

RUNAWAY NEWS

[The News Anchor]

"Power outages
are due to outdated infrastructure,"
city planner proclaims,
"We need to build
expand!
in order to meet demand
under our leader's command
we'll provide for all
throughout the land —
supply and demand!
If that means more war
I suppose that's where we stand."

Another teleprompter loop.

"Just smile and read the news!"

It's my job to share
official views
segue to sports —
national distractions
close with climate —
prevalent prevarication
tune in at five
where you'll hear
everything's just fine,

those suns will burn
until the very end of time.

Paid to propagate
perceived perception
insulate insecurities
proclaim protection
Maslow's hierarchy of needs
Poker Face Champion —
you're looking at me
concealing the hand of death
apparently that's what I do best —
expertly enunciated words
manufactured facts —
please don't quote me on that.

Don't believe them
when they tell you
there's no alternate plan —
no inhabitable planets
no parallel worlds
or enemies close at hand —
those are all just words
existing in places
other than Truth —
they want us here,
powering projects
engineering energy
digging up rocks —
toiling treachery

obliterating resources
mining the soul
out of this scorched planet —
taking it all
selling it all
before it's all too late,
convinced of your conviction
they left you
with a set of rules
skipped off
to an undisclosed location in the sky,
I've seen video —
a confidential eye witness
confirming all of this
documents
exclusive footage —
proof!
They've been keeping it from us
blinding us
distracting us
not believing in us ...

Another ship is leaving soon —

There's not much time —

I'm no conspiracy theorist
no beaked ghosts here,
I'm using my connections
secured a seat

leaving tonight —
not going to stick around
I'm going
to catch that flight.

BEAKS AND BONES

[The Archeologist]

Beaks and bones
buried beneath the stones —
the first was found
on a normal round,
average miners
doing their job
digging up minerals
sourcing our meals,
tunneled deeper
uncovered the mystery
that has become our history —
now look how far we've come
hundreds of them
exhumed from the ground
critics and skeptics
unable to hide
the things in the soil
simply don't lie —
our planet hosted others
long before we arrived,
this hot sordid air
changing geological conditions
volcanic eruptions
a plethora of disruptions
annihilated these lifeforms —
buried them here, but

no one else was around, so
we're not one-hundred percent clear

Now that we've found them
now that they're out —
we've prepared
exquisite quarters
accommodations for queens —
an afterlife for skeletons
dusted
erected
put on display —
you can visit them any day
pay your respects,
some light a candle
make a hushed request —
we've unearthed
a subtle unrest
if this is one secret,
where is the next?
I'll keep cross-referencing
looking
searching
scratching at rocks
looking for evidence
of what was here before us —
One day I'll discover
what we've yet to uncover.

DESTINY

[The Career Counselor]

It's your Identity
Your Personality
Your Version of Reality
Your Profession is everything, you see
these tests will determine
Your Destiny —

Take a clipboard
I'll be with you shortly.

LEATHERWORK

[The Tailor]

Why, yes!
I *am* a tailor
among the very best
I sew at full tilt
far faster
much quicker
than the rest

Polyester pajamas
leather overcoats —
and everything in-between,
if you know what I mean

Protective garments
or everyday wear
I'm well versed
in any textile
all fashion styles
I started in polyester
learned the tricks of the trade —
inseams
pleats
cutting on the bias
I do them all —
can't deny this!
Only Desert Vest's

very best polymers
are used here
spun here
brought to life here —
we've quite a large shop, dear

What?
Why, no!
don't be silly,
everyone knows the rule —
these soft fibers
mus'n't be worn above ground
you'll have third degree burns
a funny smell
checkered skin —
that is,
if you know
tartan
is in

Oh! Please, pardon my humor!
Yes!
certainly,
leather
is the fare you must wear
should you ever need
to face the air,
but
fresh hides
are not plentiful

not this season —
I've heard rumors
hushed whispers:
we've been low
on battle wins —
hence
no new skins,
hopefully things
will pick up again.

Absolutely!
We're equipped for any material
rations of raw hide aren't promised,
but tend to arrive
Tuesdays by nine
we clean them
degrease them
tan them
stretch them —
dry
commodify —
that perfectly prepared hide
goes for a glide
under reinforced needles
miniature inverted steeples —
each stitch
a surgical procedure
resuming a shape
it was born to make

Hey!

I know a guy
in military supply
he gets the best pelts
cuts a few loose
fattens his goose
good leather
never loses its value
nothing better
than Marred One pelts
that dermis!
Oh, the thickness I've felt!
perfect polarization —
Darwin's star student,
we're all good for something!
Marred Ones are made for these shears
and for protecting our worst fears —
nothing staves off radiation
like a Margo cappello
matching overcoat
custom gloves
I stitch them all up with love!

What size are you, hon?

I've been saving
holding back more than a few
these fit you beautifully, too!
What da'ya say?
Do we have a deal?
No use arguing
with a steal!

Hmm, I
I know the look in your eye —
Go on!
put the hide's original owner
right on out of your mind —
these things
are simply
a-part
apart
of our time —
rest assured,
nothing's a waste
all's in
its proper place,
don't feel bad
you need'n't wear it
unless your job
brings you outside,
then come see me

As I've said
I have an in
invest in quality
nothing beats those skins!

But, oh!
the polyester —
it's by far my favorite
such a delight
singing past the needle

kissing speeds of light,
following the pattern
I memorized
easily put to mind
I'm an expert —
a pro
let's get your measurements
then I'll be ready to go,
everyone deserves
to look their very best —
why would someone as classy as you
settle for less?

You'll be equally comfortable
in all varying degrees
of aridity —
not to mention
how you'll sit!
so comfortably
my garments
can't pinch
could never sinch —
why, I only make pants
which are custom fit!
And, yes -
dear, yes
I happily accept
either
cash
or check.

SUN GYPSY

[The Musician]

I ran away —
at least that's what my mother would say.
Childhood was plain
monotonous
androgynous
rules
restrictions —
dressing all the same
thinking between the lines
sheltered from suns
growing up underground
like everyone
no different
all the same —
but then
I started thinking about
Plato's allegory
the one with the cave —
I had to get out
had to leave!
Surrounded by the blind
who didn't mind,
but, I
I *had* to go somewhere —
overwhelmed
compelled

needed to leave
seeking somewhere
anywhere I could see

I swiped some clothes
filled a bag with pills
took the stairwell,
dusty
disused tunnel —
not unlike the one you used
to find me here,

By the way,
nice gear.
Blackmarket?
Or a gift from the deceased?
either way,
I'm interested in discussing a trade,
my overcoat
has seen better days
had it since the beginning
first moments under the suns —
it was ten years ago
more or less,
I climbed up
straight up to the surface
lifted the hatch —
and
they were there,
people who could see

they came, just as they said —
waited for me
exactly as they said they'd be,
in a ramshackle sun buggy
painted the same color
as copper citrine money.

Since that day
we've traveled countless miles
witnessed horrific defiles
unheard of conflict
rages above us —
battles flash in the sky
followed by storms,
debris
it's out there to see
raining down from between the suns
splinters of flight-ships —
DV ships
crashing to the sands
they sporadically appear
fresh from the thermosphere
blackened bones of soldiers
incinerated by The Marred Ones
The Ones, you're told,
are light-years away
told that battles rage —
but they're so far,

endlessly far away

Yet here they are —
I see them
fireworks erupting
in a blistering sky
meteors of metal
burning out craters of sand
supposed enemies
close at hand
I've seen a Marred One's ship
her body inside,
burnt to a crisp
hide unusable,
(or we'd 'of taken a snip)
hunks of metal
thrown from the sky
so many of our fighters
dying above us
roaring toward the ground —
but no one listens
so it doesn't make a sound.

We roam far from the forests —
those wired metal oddities,
far enough away
to dodge security
circumvent society
seeing the things
engineers fail to see —
witness battles

in the open land
obscured by plateaus
obsidian and sand
hundreds of miles
from elevator shafts
while far under the rock
families placidly stare at screens
domesticated by documentaries —
DV leadership sponsored programming,
never dreaming
the battle is growing
closing in
homing
they believe we're sending firearms
to our soldiers
stationed in faraway lands
places even more uninhabitable
than our scorched sand —
trusting those who say
the universe is bleak,
nothing is comfortable
nothing below triple-digit
on the Fahrenheit scale —
imagination is futile
you're just wailing to wail
They have it all going
going according to plan,
you just sit tight
Keep Calm, Carry On
be thankful

remember —
Desert Vest is the Best!
Patriotism.
Loyalty.
This is the soil of your birth
we could never do any hurt
never be at fault —
Truth is screened
by default,
now swallow your vitamin
and head on down your tunnel
you're late for clean-up duty
behind on your work,
questions aren't afforded
not to your kind
now
kindly,
step back in line.

That's why I'm out here!
Roaming
sweating
scrapping by on what we find
we answer to no one
but the suns.

A friend of mine
crafts instruments
from wire —
from twine,

bits allegedly stolen
twisted
re-fined
shaped into new form.

We strum them
hum along with them
make them sing
reverberate out,
create our own beat
making music
if only for the heat
surrounding this small fleet.

If you've heard of us
no doubt
you have doubt of us,
can't believe we get by:
clunky metal sand trailers
touring toward
the hazy horizon line —
avoiding tunnel doors
navigating around electrical grids
circumventing infrastructure
following invisible highways
not mapped out in advance —
symbiotic romance
outliners
renegades
gypsies under the suns

poets
mystics
always on the run,
this troupe
has been called any
and all of the above,
but nothing makes me happier
than being free —
sailing the desert sea
under these warring suns

and hope of harmony.

INFANTRY, FORGET ABOUT ME

[The Soldier]

I've only stepped off the ship
please,
give me a minute to sit
to settle down
part of me is still up there
flying around

Let me remove my gear
set it down over here
man, let me tell you —
nothing is better
than peeling off this leather

Hey,
keep this off the record,
we never spoke:
but,
wearing leather
anywhere outside of this planet
is a joke

Sure,
it's protective in deep space —
but we never leave
the ship's embrace,
not until we land

on those foreign sands —

See,
that's the thing
they tell it to everyone wrong —
because
I've yet to see *sand*
in any foreign land

Both planets I've seen
in my first tour of duty
were overgrown,
a new color
somewhere between
oxidized copper
and those malachite machines —
stalky beings
sedentary feelings
no match for a machete
and pent-up energy

That's right —
Infantry! Ho!
Battalion Two-Twenty-Two
Company Four!
Bringing vengeance
straight to the door
bagging Margos
knocking them to the floor
tracking them through the galaxy

always hunting for more.
But lately
they've been spotted here
taken down here —
were caught raiding a closed mine
way out in DV sector *nine.*
Clearly their intel's no sleuth
no Dr. Watson in a spacesuit —
but they've been landing here
and they're going to pay, dear.

This platoon
is specially trained
we win each fight
day or night
combat ready
fire our zap rifles
at just the right height
stops a Marred One's heart
stops it fast, all right —

Machine gun?
What do you mean, hon?
I haven't fired one of those
since Camp Desert Vest One
we're modernized
tech-weaponized
under strict orders
to preserve hides
no primal knives

or traditional ballistics permitted
we're unstoppable
forty-four thousand volt rifles
knocks 'um right out
keeps their hide
mint
perfect condition
then I get to come home
complete my mission.

Now if you'll excuse me,
sergeant's waving —
I have a debriefing meeting
can't keep the brass waiting

You want to wait here?
Sure, we can talk a bit more
give me a few minutes
stand over by that door.

* * *

Um, yes?
'Cuse me, I'm tryin'a pass
need to get goin'
'm supposed to be at a class —
What?
'Ne'r heard 'a ya!
don't be daft
course I shoot an 'mm-sixty!

Burn through countless barr'ls
mow'n down Margo 'ucks
destroyin' all their cargo trucks
weakening supply chains
'n such
sun's so hot on that dam' planet
our boys gonna' need more stuff!
Put that in 'yer paper
write it all up!

KIPLING'S BARON

[The Blacksmith]

Firing black to yellow
orange
then red —
iron and steel
is how I earn my bread
forging behemoths
that keep you tucked safely in bed

A delaminated line?
isn't acceptable
not at all fine —
grow the flame
heat the flux
swing with might
quenching in oil
when the time is right

Look around you —
it's all metal
damascus steel
aluminum composite
alloy flight-ships,
from pick axes
to pill bottles —
elevators
and barrack bulkheads —

it's all around your sweet
pretty
little head
all fashioned by fire
smelt by smith men
twenty-five hours a'day
here,
in the pit of the earth
hammering away

You may be able to fly past the suns,
heal the wounded
uncover Beaked Ones
but none
not a single one
would be anywhere
without my sweat
my mentor's tears —
light-years of progress
started right here,
down in this hall —
where
"Iron — Cold Iron — is master of them all."[1]

---

[1] Rudyard Kipling, "Cold Iron," in *Rewards and Fairies* (Macmillan and Co., London, 1910), 3

BROTHERHOOD OF THE BEAKED ONES

[The Preacher]

Ostrich
Veal
The Unknown
has its appeal —
the day they were found
brought forward
"discovered"
A'hem! Plundered!
we were still undercover
just a small group of us

We knew they were there
their physical remains
buried for eons
in fluorite caves
while their spirits
transverse the multi-verse
of the ill rehearsed

You see,
this hasn't always been me
but my visions began
around age twenty-three
beaked creatures
with stunted wings
on a planet with two suns

eerily like ours —
only the light was weak
one star
was quite far

They flourished
for a time
had plenty to eat
I walked with them
sat next to their seat —
they shared things
and these dreams!
They repeat
over and over
until I wanted nothing
but relief
it was impossible to sleep —

But then I went on to meet
another
and another
a group of us
an ever-widening
sect
of us
identical dreams
visions of these Beaked Ones
and what's to become of our suns.
People who dream of Them
seek us out
find us out

tell us
they were guided out

Our numbers are growing
multiplying
not plateauing
this is no cult
nothing confining
not at all conforming
we promote peace
non-violence
equal treatment of Margos —
in fact
we'd really like
to see that word go

The Marred Ones
need compassion
deserve respect —
we've had visions
seen the history of DV
time unraveled
showed itself to me:
the ones with the tough skin
they were once our kin

They started here with us,
on Desert Vest
before time registered
in consciousness,
living in caves

on the surface
all of us
until a small difference
petty argument
got the best of us.
Our ancestors
burrowed underground
left the surface
while the other group
mingled with the suns
for a few millennia
staying on DV
long enough to forever change
perfect that skin
human skin
the same variety
you shamelessly find yourself in —

I pray you sense
there's more to the story
than waging war
forging glory
taking lives to save lives
invisible irony —
can we rise above that?
You and me?
Humanity?

The Beaked Ones,
O' Revered Ones,
once warned The Marred Ones,

and they're telling us too:
we have an unstable star
agitator of the cosmos
demon doppelganger
Sun Two —
it has its eye set on you
on us
lusting for land,
infatuated
with what it can see
but
is not permitted to touch —
it broke away from the sky
began a gradual decent
content to prolong its threat

When it first shifted
took the first step
The Beaked Ones
suffered famine
didn't survive
the first climate demise —
killed off The Revered Ones,
Ones
who were once known to our own
ancient ancestors
the eldest of humankind
yours
and mine —
we left them there
to dig out our mines

never speaking of them again
redacted history
reengineered our stories
around mineral glory
far from the surface
far from the air
far from the Truth
we dug out this lair.

The Marred Ones —
their people
they got the message
more than a few
millennia ago
their people listened to the dreamers
they let it all go,
left this time bomb behind
secured galactic relocation
for their entire kind —
colonized new planets
devoured exotic cuisine

Our only true hope
is following their lead,
board a flight-ship
hit the hyper-drive
now, is the time for speed

Here —
take this pamphlet
it spells it all out —

you'll see
time
is not a running spout
and the ones in power,
won't help you out
not gonna come through
don't tell me you believe
DV government cares for you—
but, The Beaked Ones
they can speak to you too —
our group
isn't just for the few

They inspire us
encourage us
want for us
what they never had:
a way off this land
flight!
A new nest!
A planet at rest
see our grandchildren free
free from soil-dwelling deformity,
collapsed lungs
and steroid drugs
left back to history —
we believe
there's space out there for us
ready
perfectly habitable
abundant food source

one beautifully moderate
Helios
a planet in stable orbit —
we've glimpsed it
we know it!
Believe it's fair
we're going to get there
leave Desert Vest
off to the next!

The Beaked Ones
have many secrets to share!
If you're curious
perhaps you'll join us
talk with us
commune with us —
we meet every Saturday
in DV sector thirty-two
negative-floor ten
just knock like this
when you want to come in
__   *__*__*__*

TUNNEL FOUR-FIFTY, EXIT B

[The Janitor]

If you're set on standing there
kindly hand me that hose
I've just finished refilling
and I need to get back
back
down my rows

Yea, cleaning's
what they gave me —
cleaning's
what I got
didn't even bother
to test for another lot
figured
I'd leave it to luck
end up where I'ought
job's not glamorous
but
they need us
pay's not high
but
we scrape by
it's not all about money
or getting ahead
life's little joys
are all in your head

I live down in DV Sector Seventy-C
Negative Floor One-Eighty-Three
I take Tunnel Four-Fifty, Exit B
that's where we meet
every quarter ta' three

We load our gear
then ride a car
deeper
than you'll pro'ly ever be
down
to the dirtiest mine
this side of the fault line —
some kinda' essential mineral-
at least that's what they tell ya
whatever it is —
it's all the same to me,
I'm just there to clean
swab the hoses on the filters
reset all the latrines

Best part of my job
happens around lunch
all the cleaners meander
near the punch
and sometimes
she's there —
the janitor with
the long silver hair
full pouty lips

eyes that glint
catching light from the reactor,
standing there
backlit,
my heart will skip!
Janitor Number Two-Hundred-Three
Oh,
how I wish she were with me
chatting openly
sharing those stories I overhear
sitting near
holding eyes
locking stares —

She captivates
exhilarates!
I tell you,
I live for these breaks!

She said she'd been to the surface
saw the suns
traveled with gypsies
beat on some drums
no one believes her
most all of them laughed,
but she held their eyes
not the type
who easily cries —
I believe her

even if it's all just lies.

Maybe today I'll get'a chance —
sit by her
steal a glance
ask her to tell me
if she knows how to dance
let her know
she's breathtaking
in a place with no breath to take
she's intriguing
infinitely interesting
hijacked my hermit heart
'n gave me a new start —

Who cares for the suns —
as long as I get to see
Janitor Two-Hundred-Three
down off Tunnel Four-Fifty
Exit B

CLASSIFIED CATASTROPHE

[The Farmer]

Who are you?
And
who, exactly
cleared you
screened you
let you pass within?
of course,
Security is quite restricted —
impossible to get in

Do you
have credentials
sent by officials?
I need to see them
see what all this is about —
lay them on the table
let me sort this all out —
Alright
you seem legit,
no need to sit
follow me
as I walk for a bit —
So,
What is it?
What can I help you with?
Things haven't been going

not going so well
to be quite honest
perfectly frank:
it's not so swell
gone right down the tank —
'n never
not ever
it's not gonna be
our leather bank

The Farm Project's
been around,
around
along time —
half a century!
least that's
what they tell me
what I heard,
but of course
none of us
not
one of us
can ever,
never
say a word

See,
it's *their diet*!
'n you name it,
we've tried it —

administered premium vitamins
each specialty blended
Calcium Copper Titanate
C-C-T-O
thought that stuff
was good to go —
but no
killed 'em off,
had to start again —
purchase new freight
get 'em up to weight,
so, naturally
we tried
magnesium sulfate

And man,
I just wanna say
that stuff
let me tell ya
it really
really
tastes great —
my personal preference
rate it top rate
devour it up
each lunch break
but can you believe it,
even that
wouldn't take

Vital vitamin digestion:

's been
our biggest question
these Margos —
they must
have some kind
of funky design
'n the inside —
foreign features
within these —
these
very fragile creatures,
something preventing —
restraining absorption
causing coagulation
what a frustration!
We haven't had any luck
on this here operation.

No,
it's not the sedatives
they're working —
doing just fine
simply not practical
to have them up
stomping
mumbling
moving around
we're doing fine
perfectly fine
they're all in place
arranged neatly in line

row after row of Margo
intravenously cared for

But
we can't sustain them
can't keep 'um alive
there's something extra they need
need to thrive —
but
The Farm Project
has never passed phase one:
top secret
classified catastrophe —
some days it feels
like the walls are closing in around me
a profusion of pressure
long became
my constant censure
inherited the obsession
thanks ta' my profession

We need more time
time to get it right
it hasn't been easy
no easy plight —
turned into a bit
of a Marred money-pit,
'n certainly
didn't happen overnight

We're vying for capital

extension after extension
additional funding
subsidized subsidies
bail outs
invest —
it could pay out!
This Project is worth trillions
once we've kicked the kinks out
ironed all the problems out
flushed some new ideas out
although it's been bleak
there could be a turnabout
but, ultimately
I can't get out —
not until I get my payout.

TENURED DEATH
[The Professor]

Stretching young minds
through underground mines
and stratigraphic lines
stalagmites
stalactites
caves of selenite,
spatially varying density
your time spent with me
is all about Geology

Class begins promptly
on the dot —
right at eight
I respectfully ask
you not be late,
find your seat,
prepare to notate

Exams are expected
expect them expectantly —
Plan accordingly
Study habits are key —
take it from me,
Stay on your toes
Put aside algebraic woes —
we have our own foes,

Before you know it
you'll have graduated
a scholar
white collar
working in your field
making a dollar
but first
you have to pass —
make it through me
if you want that degree
that ticket to the top tests
here
your fate precariously rests —
study hard!
impress me
remind me
that teaching is where
I'm meant to be

Grading papers
rife with trivial answers
throwaway responses
abhorrent explanation —
I want to see genius!
despise handing out a B
sometimes I question
why I tested into this life for me,
maybe if I'd only
scored higher in Chemistry
I could have avoided

this tedious monotony

I used to enjoy it
really
I did,
halcyon days
with the students
the kids
my first year instructing
a blessing
a calling —
Now though,
it's changed
I'm bored
listless,
how many more years
can I really
honestly
do this?
Semester
after semester
teaching those
who have a chance —
take Destiny
out for a dance,
an opportunity
a pass —
test into a higher class
experimenting
developing

leading your peers
inflicting great change
across an expanse of years —
not stuck in a classroom
robotically passing the years.
Most can't appreciate
time's perspective
in such youthful state.

You could end up
in engineering
peering
down long ventilation shafts
controlling up-ward draughts
with rudders —
flaps
synchronizing platforms of fans
turning
turning
oscillating
whirling
calibrated
calculated —
all set
to precisely one speed
with you,
young student,
there at the lead
Ah!
Brevity:

a private showing
just for me,
sitting here
muddling
puddling
toward tenured death
running low on breath —
coming to terms
with Regret —
hoping you'll remember me,
Professor of Geology,
when you get to see
whatever it is
you're meant to be.

FINDING TIME

[The Astrophysicist]

You want more time.
Sure,
We all do.
What else is new?
You're with your friends
not wanting the good times to end —
or your project is due,
you didn't get enough time
not enough to make it through
So you're begging Kronos for more
squeezing every moment
procrastination
barely courting asphyxiation
you make it with seconds to spare
constantly on the search
for spare change
in the form of minutes
seconds
split hairs
coaxing time to a drawl
as you roll out of bed,
on with your routine
assuming life
is just as it Should Be
as long as
everything's done on time

Did you know
that if you move a clock
closer to a mountain
time slows down?
Physics, my friend —
that's the short and sweet
sure, get a new apartment in DV-eight
the mountains are above head
the rent's a good rate —
save yourself a half-a-second a week
it'll add up faster than you think

Quantifiable.
Undeniable.

Yep, I'm here six days a week:
tracking comets
asteroid fields
monitoring gamma radiation
running equations —

What did you say your story is about?
Is this a piece for the nightly news?

Or are you from some extremist group?

I've done those interviews before
and frankly
I'm not looking for more

Our suns are both stable
nothing has changed,
everything is exactly the same —
yes,
that is my repeated refrain
the data
just hasn't changed

People and their conspiracy —
Please!
Just let it be.

Leave the science to scientists
we're fully funded
by the government, you see

If you have time to entertain an apocalypse
then it's time to get back to work.
You have plenty of hours in your day.

Forget about finding time under mountains
you have it in change —

Be wary how you spend it
publish what you dare,
there are no heroes in philosophy
no soothsayers
in science

The Data simply supports this.

Now kindly leave your recorder
throw it in the can by the door
see yourself out
we don't have anything left to talk about.

PATIENT PRIVACY

[The Physician]

How are you today?
How do you feel?
any wheezing
or heavy breathing?
What is your aliment
Name your presumptive ill?
Let's begin
with symptoms
List them all out
Tell me,
Have you ever suffered from gout?
Tell me
Tell me
What brought it about?
How old were you
when your gall bladder
was taken out?

Your history is crucial
vital, on key —
my evaluation is based
on more than what I see,
So, please,
be perfectly candid with me
no medical monstrosity
can intimidate me

and, of course,
I respect
patient privacy.

I've seen everything,
everything under these suns
'been a primary care physician
since nineteen-eighty-one —
Hippocratic Analgesic
I'm not opposed
to comfortably numb
like children sucking thumbs
pain pills preferred,
four to one
but
that's only going to take you so far
you'll
build up a tolerance
want me to increase your allowance
fast forward to the end
you're incapacitated
alienated
meanwhile I'm under-rated
an automaton 'script pad —
if that's what you need
you better zip it up and leave
I'm a physician who believes
in treating the problem
not masking dis-ease

After all these years

examining bodies
from across Desert Vest
analyzing x-rays
giving new medicines a test,
the only thing
that's really mystified me
got my head in a spin —
my colleagues —
none of us can seem to win
progress on providing a prognosis —

What has been happening to our infantry?!

My patients who've
traveled across galaxies
skipped through light-years
appear to all suffer
from radiological fallout,
varying degrees
of brain cell knockout
large portions of grey matter
have gone dark,
no longer a factor
their senses don't respond
in an entirely appropriate manner.

The decommissioned
the newly un-enlisted
so often present
describing stomach upset
we run tests

uncover digestive deformities
presumably
from consuming alien anomalies —
when quizzed
they can't recall
have no idea
zero recollection
about anything surrounding the mission
they honestly endeavor —
I see them struggle
strain to remember
what they ate
or where they got their plate:
my peers and I
simply can't understand
why none have memory
at their command.

If you meet one —
out interviewing
quoting
whatever it is you're doing —
should you happen to spy
a former G.I.
retired guy
give them your ear
don't simply sigh
and pass them by
surely one of them remembers
their digestive adventures —
then pay me a visit

please don't delay
I want to help them —
there must be a way.

CANARY IN A COAL MINE

[The Miner]

Salt of the earth
dig up everything it's worth
this is the land
of supply and demand.
You like it this way
prefer it stay
Me?
on my way to the grave,
technological advancements
simply aren't headed this way
priority is military —
what else is there to say
resources are thin
but you've plenty of young men
swinging picks
loading rock
lighting the fuse
hearing the pop
now back to work!
diggers
miners
shoveling for miles
bend with the knees
lift with the back —
sooner have a heart attack
every muscle

tendon
screaming to defile
lay the ax down
casually drown
each swing a wager
a scream
a razor,
how much longer
until I stagger
black out
knock out
tap out
sucking at air
that's never promised to be there
somehow I make it
survive another day

Sundays I cringe
by Friday I weep
unimaginable pain
building throughout the week
Saturday: I want nothing
but sleep —
only,
I've been voyaging
hiking
exploring
leaving my sector —
Death renders in vector
my time will soon come,

It comes for everyone

Keep Saturdays Fun!
although I know no one
brave enough to accompany me
leave this hell with me
explore other realities —
I hike through entire communities
barracks of industries
people who have no concept of me
going about lives
in complete apathy
never considering
imagining
believing
they could leave
walk around with me
tour the property
blend in seamlessly —
it's all congruent
to social affluency
simply copy what you see —
that's the trick
to normality
escape your grind
go behind the bourgeoisie line
nose about —
gives me something
to think about
wrap my mind throughout

pacify the time-clock
quiet arthritic bouts
shoveling ore
wanting more
forgetting about
my lot
my rank
this job
my fears
I've only got
a few more years
black lung
it'll kill ya,
eight 'ta one
I'm bound to catch it
any day
they'll diagnose me
sell me my grave
that's one I've got to stave

I shouldn't tell you
but
I've met someone new
way out in DV Seventy-Two
she works in testing
job placement consulting
I'm unsure where I'd be going
but I'm willing
don't need goading
I'd even leave Desert Vest

shoot me into space
pink salt mines
leave this world behind —
If don't get the job
if she closes the door
I'll hike around
find some more
Brimstone and basements
are not for me,
stacked in the cellar
struggling to see
when there's a universe —
an entire universe
out there waiting
palpitating
it could be all mine for the taking —
subterranean servitude
chronic coxalgia
strength depleting each day,
it isn't meant for me
can't be for me
not when there's more to see
endless tunnels
and only one canary
still able to breathe

GOODNIGHT

[The Leader]

Join me on the captain's deck
precisely at five-fifty-five
according to calculations
we're nearing the Zenith of Time
Sun Two will come to rest
right on top of Desert Vest —
Boom!
Goodnight!
No need to turn out the light
this, my friend
is the very last flight —
toast
delight
we made it
we're free
off to the colony.
Cheers to me —
I've always been a negotiator
political hostage taker
rebel rain maker —
Desert Vest is led by the best
generations of advice
Machiavellian pie slice —
my, oh my
that power has been nice
grandma's entire family tree

ends at me,
their initiatives
bequeathed to me
forests of electrical trees
monopoly on utilities
endless commodities!
Oceans of magnesium mines
as far as the seismographer can see
all of it mine
Desert Vest is owned by me
reports to me
kneels to me
respected throughout the galaxy

Imagine my dismay when *they* came to me
talking of Beaked Ones
and pathways of suns —
I always understood planets
circulate
while suns
stayed somewhat
firmly in place —
but they stirred me
their tiny eyes didn't shine at me
I know deception — but
they didn't offer it to me
I wanted to doubt,
but their quacky calculations checked out
some supposed deity
bag of bones prophecy

led them to their tireless inquest
cosmic pathways
trajectories
spatial highways

Do you see what I'm saying?

They predicted The End —
Collusion with Sun Two
Hello, Four Horsemen
it's through
all true
and happening quite soon
prompted our exodus
and, might I say,
this stately view —
Oh!
The inferno is due!
in one...
two...

Ah! There it goes —
right on cue

Ka-Pew!!

Spare no salt from your eyes
there's nothing to fear
for a select few of us,
my circle

my crew
and
the people I admire, including
you —

I've built us a new home base
underground
fortified
pacified
leave the old wars behind
start anew
F' the suns
and DV too
we're made for something better
something new —
The colony's host planet
boasts moderate temperatures
a stable core
an intact ozone —
need I tell more?

Yes,
we'll be underground
the surface dwellers
have expanded shore to shore —
every corner of this universe
is already at full capacity
No Vacancy
my pilots confirmed this for me
(living is a luxury

it's never been free)
so I bought the colony
on Planet Fifty-Three
located in the middle of Galaxy Vee
this place
is prime real estate —
the populace was oblivious
letting it sit in disuse,
how obtuse!
It is perfect for our use.

Outside our boundary
on the surface, that is
the planet's largest regime
is driven purely by greed
coveting metals
not discovered in their soils
they were easily bought
it didn't take a whole lot
Ha! —
Recall our record year
gross capital margin
nothing beat DV production
increased blue collar jobs —
machine gun barrel bartering chips
metal is metal
the shape, trivial
they melt it down later
forge what they will,
financing my projects

keeping us in new technology —
DV goods
are an accepted form
of intergalactic currency.

But, alas —
my own legacy can't end with this
there is something bigger than this
new slate
open gate
apocalypses look fortuitous
from this vantage point
our view
The Phoenix
brand new —
Let's forget about Margos
and supply embargos —
we no longer require skins,
so why tell them where we've been?

Help me as I step forward
advise the populous
shape the state
the colony needs leadership —
not just anyone
can preside
it takes foresight
and a certain bit
of military might —
but what I'm missing

is someone who can write
Official Bulletins
lead them with your tale
Pied Piper down the rat trail
your positive spin —
they believe you're a good person, within

We're starting fresh
entirely anew
and I have just the role
the perfect position
The Job for You
you're going to be in charge
while I duck out of view
take in other cultures
read science fiction
poetic depictions,
can you believe
this planet has a library system!
Surface level cities
feature thriving arts sectors —
vibrant visual scenes
mellifluous metaphors
and stages bursting
with people who've rehearsed
and rehearsed —
At last
the time has come —
happy doomsday, everyone.

I've shelved all my volumes

of algebraic equations
geological notations
astrophysical observations —

Who cares anymore about cosmic vibrations?

This ruler
is going on vacation.

ACKNOWLEDGMENTS

"The Tree Builder" first appeared in *Eye to the Telescope: The Science Fiction and Fantasy Association Online Journal of Speculative Poetry,* Issue 25, July 2017, edited by John Reinhart

"The Tree Builder" was published in <u>The 2018 Rhysling Anthology</u> by the Science Fiction and Fantasy Poetry Association, edited by Linda D. Addison

ABOUT ATMOSPHERE PRESS

Atmosphere Press is an independent, full-service publisher for books in genres ranging from nonfiction to fiction to poetry, with a special emphasis on being an author-friendly approach to the challenges of getting a book into the world. Learn more about what we do at atmospherepress.com.

We encourage you to check out some of Atmosphere's latest releases, which are available at Amazon.com and via order from your local bookstore:

Unorthodoxy, a novel by Joshua A.H. Harris
A User Guide to the Unconscious Mind, nonfiction by
    Tatiana Lukyanova
The Sky Belongs to the Dreamers, a picture book by
    J.P. Hostetler
To the Next Step: Your Guide from High School and
    College to The Real World, nonfiction by Kyle
    Grappone
The George Stories, a novel by Christopher Gould
No Home Like a Raft, poetry by Martin Jon Porter
Mere Being, poetry by Barry D. Amis
The Traveler, a young adult novel by Jennifer Deaver
Breathing New Life: Finding Happiness after Tragedy,
    nonfiction by Bunny Leach
Oscar the Loveable Seagull, a picture book by Mark
    Johnson
Mandated Happiness, a novel by Clayton Tucker
The Third Door, a novel by Jim Williams
The Yoga of Strength, a novel by Andrew Marc Rowe
They are Almost Invisible, poetry by Elizabeth Carmer

Let the Little Birds Sing, a novel by Sandra Fox Murphy

Carpenters and Catapults: A Girls Can Do Anything Book, children's fiction by Carmen Petro

Spots Before Stripes, a novel by Jonathan Kumar

Auroras over Acadia, poetry by Paul Liebow

Channel: How to be a Clear Channel for Inspiration by Listening, Enjoying, and Trusting Your Intuition, nonfiction by Jessica Ang

Gone Fishing: A Girls Can Do Anything Book, children's fiction by Carmen Petro

Owlfred the Owl, a picture book by Caleb Foster

Love Your Vibe: Using the Power of Sound to Take Command of Your Life, nonfiction by Matt Omo

Transcendence, poetry and images by Vincent Bahar Towliat

Leaving the Ladder: An Ex-Corporate Girl's Guide from the Rat Race to Fulfilment, nonfiction by Lynda Bayada

Adrift, poems by Kristy Peloquin

Letting Nicki Go: A Mother's Journey through Her Daughter's Cancer, nonfiction by Bunny Leach

Time Do Not Stop, poems by William Guest

Dear Old Dogs, a novella by Gwen Head

Bello the Cello, a picture book by Dennis Mathew

How Not to Sell: A Sales Survival Guide, nonfiction by Rashad Daoudi

Ghost Sentence, poems by Mary Flanagan

That Scarlett Bacon, a picture book by Mark Johnson

Such a Nice Girl, a novel by Carol St. John

Makani and the Tiki Mikis, a picture book by Kosta Gregory

What Outlives Us, poems by Larry Levy

Winter Park, a novel by Graham Guest

That Beautiful Season, a novel by Sandra Fox Murphy

ABOUT THE AUTHOR

Christina Loraine is a creative powerhouse who resides far enough outside of Chicago to see the stars at night with her son and husband. She studied philosophy at Western Illinois University and then pursued a headhunting career in Atlanta while moonlighting as an artist. Christina is a self-taught painter who continues to exhibit at galleries and festivals; she also enjoys inspiring others in informal classroom settings. Always penning poems of speculative worlds infused with literary overtones, she's finally gotten around to making the writer part of her Artist/Writer title official with this first book.

[ChristinaLoraine.com]

CPSIA information can be obtained
at www.ICGtesting.com
Printed in the USA
FFHW021608240719
53855086-59545FF